Titbits

G000112483

SHORT STORIES
BY PETER VINKIL

AUSTIN MACAULEY PUBLISHERS™

LONDON • CAMBRIDGE • NEW YORK • SHARJAH

A CIP catalogue record for this title is available from the British Library.

ISBN 9781528931526 (Paperback)
ISBN 9781528931533 (Kindle e-book)
ISBN 9781528951326 (ePub e-book)

www.austinmacauley.com

First Published (2019)
Austin Macauley Publishers Ltd
25 Canada Square
Canary Wharf
London
E14 5LQ

Black Shock

'Sanity is only that which is within the frame of reference of conventional thought.'

– Erich Fromm

What is done is done and I do not expect you to believe what I am about to pen, indeed my very senses reject the evidence as I now communicate it to you. I confess my sin and will endeavour to tell my story in as lucid a manner as I can command, 'but' I assure you I am not mad and these events are not some terrible demonic dream.

My name is Selkie Denison. Born in the Orkney parish of St Ola, in the town of Kirkwall. From an early age, I had a tenderness for animals which my now dead parents indulged by buying me various creatures like rabbits and chickens, which I would look after and was never so happy as when my attention was directed to tending them.

I married at a relatively early age and was happy to find that my husband, Alex, was of a similar disposition regarding animals to myself, and we soon had several pets, although our first house was small with only a compact little back yard. Alex was not what you would call very bright but he was loyal and generally did what I wanted and what he was told, which I think suited us both.

While my career as a minor council official and then to junior political roles progressed, we moved into a larger detached home on a large and fairly secluded plot. The house, I found out, was a converted building that used to be an old pumping station. I noticed it had a few rather unusual Gothic features on the exterior which, though somewhat chilling, seemed to hold an attraction for me. We were told it originally had a very deep cellar which housed the pump mechanism, but this had been largely boarded over and a wine cellar created above. It was at this time we added a small terrier puppy to our menagerie of creatures. We called this new addition Gordon and he had a totally jet black coat of short shiny hair and bright little eyes.

For many who have cherished an affection for a faithful and canine companion, I need not explain the intensity of the bond and contentment derived from this. There is something substantial in the love of an animal that is in stark contrast to the all too often paltry and superficial or doubtful friendship of many human friends and companions.

We also took on a part time home help around this time. Her name was Morag Phoneutria. She was fairly short and stocky in appearance with wisps of greying hair curls glancing around her face. I believe she came from Central or maybe South America. I had used my position, and somewhat illicitly helped her get a work visa for which she was most appreciative, enabling us to gain a loyal and cheap to employ servant. Mo, as we came to call her, was a pleasant enough individual who in addition to her other tasks took to looking after the welfare of the animals as required. She could speak and understand English well enough to get by, but would generally keep quietly in the background and just uncomplainingly tend to her tasks.

Our contentment did not last however. Over time, my general temperament deteriorated due in no small part to the demon drink. The evil spirit of my intemperance slowly but surely began to darken my personality. At length, I would sometimes display personal violence to Alex, and even the pets were made to suffer by my change of disposition as I consciously neglected and ill-treated them. For Gordon, however, I still seemed to have some affection and regard which prevented me from maltreating the attentive little creature.

I was, however, successful at masking my personality change in my public life, and only Alex and Mo were aware of the dark alter ego in me which could surface. This was, in truth though, only a catalyst for the events leading to my current plight as this account of events will testify to.

The Hairdresser Appointment

I remember strange and ominous circumstances started to occur on one particular afternoon. I remember I had finished my official council duties, and I was dropped off by Alex to my weekly appointment with my hairstylist.

'In my job, image is the key to success, and so one must always try to look one's best when projecting the desired character.'

It had been a fine day but there was a cold wind that had just come up. I noticed this was causing a tree to make a scraping sound as its fingery branches were blown against the shop's brick wall. I entered the salon and was presently beckoned to come over and sit down by my hairstylist Guido Gaula. Guido started tending to my hair and presently he produced a large can of scented styling mousse. Spraying it onto his palm it foamed up like whipped cream, and he proceeded to quiff up my hair so it looked like a cow's horns.

I looked in the mirror and for a split second saw a blooded red Lucifer like image of my dead mother's face staring back at me, her lips curled to a sinister smile, just for a split second, and then almost instantly my true features reappeared on the mirror's reflection.

What this ghastly mental imagery meant, I confess eluded me and it presently removed itself from my thoughts as Guido proceeded with his combing and styling.

Guido suddenly and out of the blue said, "I think real life is overrated. Why do you suppose we are here?"

Rachael the young trainee with bright pink hair and safety-pin in her nose who was sweeping the floor replied, "I'm here because I had to walk here man. So when are you gonna give me a shoe allowance then?"

Ignoring this, Guido continued, "No, no I mean why are we here on Earth, alive? I mean why are we anywhere, why do we exist?"

Rachael thought for a second and then replied, "Because we wos born and because Earth can support life an all that."

Guido sniggering, "Well you're the smart one, ain't you! Just forget it, I will, and get on with the hair, and you had better get Mrs Mason her cup of tea." He glanced around at old Mrs Mason, who had bits of silver foil spiking in all directions on her head, and gave her a little wave; to which she responded with a wide grin.

When Guido had nearly finished with the mousse, a smile curling at the edge of his mouth, he remarked, "Mousse, mousse, it's such a comical word. It's styling foam but they all call it mousse," pausing a moment and with an amused grin he continued, "Mickey mousse." He laughed and said, "There, all done-ski; you look beautiful!"

Rachael yelled from the store cupboard, "Guido can I go at half past as me boyfriend Lloyde wants to take me out later."

Guido replied back, "Lazy girl! You can go at quarter to five, no earlier. And don't let him in the shop if he is eating one of those smelly, spicy filled wrap things he likes. Last time the mucky little bugger dropped half of it on the floor, and all the hair you should have cleared up ended up sticking to it. Stank like a blooming Turkish shish kebab in here for hours!"

Turning to his audience of customers, he continued, "You just can't get the staff nowadays," he said contemptuously, shaking his head in mock disapproval. With the preening complete, all neatly quaffed, curled, volumised and oiled, credit card out I paid over a suitable financial remuneration for Guido's hairstyling artistry, plus flattery, and departed the salon.

A Coffee and Cake

I had arranged for Alex to pick me up after my hairdresser's appointment so we could go to the coffee shop in the town centre. My afternoon was free and I wanted to get some ideas for an important party speech that I needed to pen within the next week or so.

We got to the coffee shop around 4:15pm, it was still light outside but the chill wind felt colder than before, so we decided to retreat inside instead of sitting at one of the little round bistro tables outside.

Alex went up and ordered our coffees with a couple of pieces of spice cake. The barista prepared the drinks and brought them with the cake to our table.

"What does anyone need in life?" I asked.

Alex replied, "Love, my dear!!" with an amused smile, cocking his eyebrow and taking a sip of his frothy cappuccino.

"No! I am serious, what people need is a purpose. For 'political purposes' anyway," I said.

"Why can't love be a purpose?" Alex asked.

"Because it's an emotion, stupid boy. Now get serious, this speech is important and I have got to come up with a suitable hook to get their attention," I said.

I picked up my caffè latte and took a sip, had a nibble of my cake and leaned back in the chair.

'Politicians are either part of the solution or part of the problem. When they can be both, it's a secure job for life.'

Alex gobbled down his piece of cake. "Oh! This tastes heavenly… Delicious," he said between bites. As the crumbs fell down his front, he brushed them off with quick swishes of his hand. We chatted for a while as I assembled thoughts in my mind to include for my forthcoming speech.

'The sorcery of the politician is to slyly pilfer as much as they can get for themselves and in return conjure up for the people elusive sugar coated empty falsehoods of future hope and happiness.'

My smart phone rang to life with my downloaded ring tune. I picked it out of my handbag and answered. It was Myfanwy (Fanny) from my constituency office. There had apparently been some minor problem, with campaign money allegedly being used for other purposes and she was panicking. After listening to her whining and fretting, I interrupted.

"Listen," I said sternly, "We are a team and there's no 'U' in 'team' Fanny, and there's no 'I', either. So if you're not on the team, and I'm not on the team, then nobody's on the bloody team, now pull yourself together!! There is no problem with the money; it is all fine. Now listen to me, we will sort it out tomorrow, OK!"

"Yes, Counsellor Denison," she replied meekly.

"Right, good girl," I said and disconnected the call.

Heaving a sigh, I leaned back in the chair again and remarked sedately, "It's just one bloody problem after another one with her!"

At this point, the coffee shop gradually seemed to darken and the vision of my devil mother I had seen at the hairdresser's appeared again before me, her lips curled to that same sinister smile. I found that I was transfixed to my chair and unable to move. My heart started pounding and palpitating in my bosom and I felt a slight nausea as my anxiety increased. The gruesome image now floated closer towards me. The phantom positioned itself beside my ear and whispering it said, "Selkie, my dear, I am so proud of you and how much you have achieved." Elevating back a little now and in a superior tone, the ghostly image continued, "It's Megan, your mother come to talk to you."

Pointing at me with its scraggy finger and raising its voice a little it continued, "When you learn something, your brain physically changes. Did you know that? Connections are made and strengthened and other connections fade away, you can appreciate that can you!" Levitating around until it was beside me, the ghastly apparition moved its arm around my back and resting its bony red fingers on my shoulder it continued. "Now your toxic actions over time have lost you your moral traction, and a terrible future has nearly caught up with you. Unless you make amends, it will soon be time for you to pay."

The hideous creature's warning meant nothing to me, after all what could I have possibly done that was evil or wrong in any way. Now, fear is a powerful energy and that is what was pulsating through my veins now. With my fright senses being well and truly engaged, you could say I was in full panic status now. In my mind I was screaming out, 'Get away from me you evil bitch, you're not my bloody mother!!!' It's funny though, the ghostly creature did seem somewhat familiar.

The apparition had, by this time, levitated in front of me and reached out her withered arms as if to embrace my body. In my panic I loudly farted (broke wind), which mightily amused the ghastly creature, and as it laughed at my embarrassment, the dreadful apparition dispersed and the light returned into the room. I think I must have fainted at this point. I woke up to find Alex holding my head in his arms in an accident and emergency cubical. After ringing for the emergency services, Alex decided to take me to the local hospital himself as there were no ambulances available as usual.

After a while, I am not sure how long, a Dr Mack came in and had a quick glance at some notes. He muttered to himself a second or two and then said in a firm Scottish accent, "How are yer feeling now?"

I replied, "I've got a bit of a headache and my stomach aches a bit but aside from that I feel fine, thank you."

"Good, good," he replied. "Now can you tell me exactly what led up to you fainting?"

I explained that all we were doing was having our coffee and spice cake, then time seemed to stand still with everyone around me motionless, and then the ghastly demonic image appeared. I did not go into detail about my encounter being my mother for fear of sounding completely mad, and merely stated that my mouth went dry, my feeling of anxiety and having heart palpitations. After this, a feeling of drowsy light headedness. Alex had told them I had a red flush coming over my skin and face, and shortly after I just felt faint and passed out.

"I am sorry, doctor, I must sound rather stupid and idiotic," I said rather sorrowfully.

"Noo! Not at all," he tenderly assured me. "It's rare, but it sounds to me like yer may have had a mild dose of 'Myristicin' poisoning. Yer can find it in nutmeg, which would likely have been present in that spice cake yer had... If the amount of nutmeg were high enough, and in combination with the stimulant effects of the coffee, that would give a logical explanation of yer symptoms, heart palpitations, hallucinations, visions and the like."

"But Alex didn't suffer any ill effects," I said.

"Perhaps his piece of cake had a normal, harmless amount of nutmeg in it," the Dr replied. "In any case, the council food inspectors can have a wee look into it."

"What we will do is keep an eye on yer vital signs, blood pressure, pulse, temperature etc. for a wee while, and if you remain stable yer can go home. You will be safe in the hands of Nurse Benevolent," he gestured towards the rather short and stocky nurse standing nearby. "Oh and if yer keep seeing wee imaginary beasties, water down the whisky a bit!!" he said as a witty afterthought; not that I found this particularly amusing.

'I drink because I have problems and chemically speaking, alcohol is a solution.'

Nurse Benevolent remembered that we went to school together, so we were able to have a pleasant conversation about old times. She still had her head of frizzy ginger hair, going a bit grey now though. Her Christian name was Kerry, but because of the hair her nick name was 'curly', which was a bit unfortunate as her surname when she was a schoolgirl was Willies.

'Willy being a term many women use in front of males because they don't wish to appear to be common slutty tarts by calling their appendage by some other slang expression.'

It's funny, I remember her cousin was known as Dolly or rather 'Dolly the sheep' as she was carrying on with a hill farmer. She used to be a good time girl, as I remember. I don't recall her actual name but I think she became some sort of a nun.

To the Pub for a Drink or Two

I was released from the hospital later that evening and decided I would walk back home. I had earlier sent Alex off to do some errands for me, and ignoring Dr Mack's advice, I stopped off to have a drink in the Old Victoria Tavern. By now it must have been about 9.30 or 10pm and it was dark and cold outside. The pub was a bit of a dump as I remember, with a faint odour of stale beer and stinking feet, but I wanted a drink and it was on my route home. I ordered a glass of red wine and took it to a small corner table where a nearby radiator was emitting a warming glow of heat. The medicinal effects of the alcohol soon started to relax and put me at ease after the day's events. I aimlessly surveyed the room which had the usual décor of old pubs. I soon finished my drink and got another.

At some point, I did see there was a small black creature creeping about the edge of the room, with bright little eyes. I could not tell exactly what it was as it was keeping in the shadows, making itself scarcely noticeable. In any case its presence did not unduly

17

trouble me, and everyone else just seemed to ignore the little animal.

Having had my few drinks I wrapped my scarf around my neck, got up and headed back home.

Gordon's Foreboding Injury

It must have been about midnight when I got back and the street lights were piercing the dark sky. My breath coiled and evaporated as it escaped out to cool air above my scarf.

I staggered slightly unsteadily as I got back to the house, and let myself in. The hall light was on but the rest of the house was dark. I was feeling a little light headed so went to the kitchen for a glass of water, but in so doing I managed to tread on Gordon who was camouflaged in the blackness. The animal let out a panicked yelp and its clawed paw somehow tangled in my tights, scraping into my leg. In a fit of rage, I swiftly and forcefully kicked the poor creature and it flew and impacted against the tiled wall. There was a sickly unhealthy thud, a single pained yelp and he fell silent on the floor. Alex, upon hearing the commotion came downstairs and hesitantly headed towards the kitchen.

He came in and switching on the light screamed, "You maniac! What have you done! God damn you to hell woman! What have you done!"

I didn't expect for Alex to act in such an emotional way as it was totally out of character, and though my senses were somewhat dimmed I think I screamed back.

"Get normal for god's sake, or I will kill you!" or some such utterance.

When I got over my initial panic, I was still angry, even angry with Alex. I had the feeling he would let me down somehow as I had inflicted the terrible injury on our poor Gordon.

The energy of anger is what was pulsing through me now. I suppose you could say my berserk button was well and truly pressed. Alex, seeing my distress, told me to calm down and to go up to bed and he would see to the dog. I dutifully staggered up the stairs to the bedroom to subdue my panic and to sleep off my slight inebriation.

Alex put a dressing around Gordon's head and wrapped him in a blanket. Nothing more could be done until Mo arrived in the morning and she took him to the vet's for treatment. The impact had crushed in a part of his skull and one eye had to be removed, which was replaced by a shiny marble like prosthetic. His face was also slightly distorted by the injury, but he recovered. The dog would now flee or dart and hide as best he could under the stairs, in fear, whenever he saw me ever afterwards in or around the house. Poor Gordon was actually quite old by now and died about six months or so later.

Mo also became rather nervous and uneasy around me as I think back. I remember I was rather angry with Mo. I had the feeling she would betray me and possibly tell the veterinary practice I had inflicted the terrible injury on our poor Gordon. Alex had simply told her Gordon's injury was caused by a fall, but she didn't really believe him.

I confess I felt some pangs of guilt for what I had done to our faithful companion for some time after this, but that regret eventually faded.

Myfanwy's Betrayal

Over the next few months, things deteriorated substantially politically, and it was only through my superior will, intellect and determination that I kept my position and fought off my many political adversaries' attacks. I must admit this did cause my alcohol consumption to rise, as I found I desired its medicinal qualities more than ever now.

'Economic reality will always win in the end, unless politics and creative accounting have anything to do with it.'

There were also 'a few casualties' during this period. Myfanwy had decided she would no longer give me her support, and attempted to discredit me with my political party by the submission of a backstabbing accusation about expenses payments and the like. This came to nothing however, as I had made sure I kept my expenses strictly within the rules laid down by the parliamentary system, which was surprisingly accommodating, even if some payments may have been construed in some lights as being greedy, excessive or maybe not a justified or acceptable use of taxpayer's money morally or otherwise. It was, of course, also to my assistance that my peers were drinking from the same expenses trough as myself so to speak. To condemn me would be to condemn them also.

Obviously, because of her treachery, the bitch MyFanwy had to have an example made of her to prevent other betrayers coming forward. She had to go, and go she did.

'Politicians do not do underhand things, unless it's absolutely necessary.'

This is totally unrelated to her dismissal, but I did hear that she met with an unfortunate accident. She was leaving work and it was late in the evening and raining heavily outside, but as Fanny had no coat, she slit a hole in the base and sides of the green plastic carrier she had on her, and slipped it over her head like a sort of poncho giving some protection from the rain. Emblazoned on it in large white lettering across her chest was the upside down slogan 'A bag for life' and across her back 'Wear me out and you can swap me for a new one'. A cruel person may have thought that was rather appropriate.

Apparently what happened next was that she fell and landed head first down a large storm drain, which 'evidently' had a faulty manhole grill cover over it. The coroner said she must have hit her head as she fell and then drowned in a foot or so of stinking and rotten waste water at the bottom. I believe the police may have informed me, or possibly interviewed me about poor

Fanny's tragic mishap. It's funny, Fanny always had this phobia about holes, small holes as I recall. Trypophobia it's called. I remember I once waved a crumpet in front of her face and she went into a complete state of mental lunacy. Her fear of holes didn't do her any good when she fell down that big old storm drain though! Tragic though this accident was for Fanny, it did prove expedient for me when a separate enquiry investigated the party expenses records some time later.

'If you can't say anything good about people, maybe you could say lots of really bad things instead.'

Morag was another casualty and she departed around the time when Gordon finally died. At this stage, I wasn't particularly sad to be dispensing with her services. As I said, I always had the feeling she would betray me at some point and tell that veterinary nurse that I had inflicted the terrible injury on our poor Gordon. I am not too sure what happened to Morag after leaving our employment, but in any case she disappeared from our little family. Possibly she may have got deported? In any case, our menagerie of little creatures for her to look after was now somewhat depleted.

Alex had come across Dave the hamster who had keeled over and died a day or two earlier. Alex removed his little brown furry corpse from his small cage and took it to show me. I dutifully agreed I would dispose of the poor little creature somewhere suitable in the garden. I recall I wasn't really in the mood to bury little Dave at the time, so upon Alex's departure I picked up his cold and by now stiff dead little body by one of his tiny feet, and with my finger and thumb I gently flung it out into the garden through the nearby open window. As I was watching little Dave aerodynamically flying to his final resting place, unfortunately a seagull snatched him in mid-air. I did feel a little guilty that I hadn't buried Dave, after seeing his little body ripped apart for a seagull snack, but I did console myself that he had served a useful purpose with his death. It's what he would have wanted, I am sure. This, unfortunately, left us with just a couple of large white rats called Bob and Dylan, who were thankfully scampering around still fit and healthy for now.

Gordon's Doppelgänger
During the next few months things seemed to improve somewhat both politically, and at home with my

drinking returning to a moderate level. The party was doing well in the polls and victory in the forthcoming local elections, although nothing is certain, looked likely.

Our local party leader and a great and respected politician, The Right Honourable Sir Richard Mørkhudet Head, had just visited our constituency offices and the whole mood and atmosphere was optimistic, which seemed to improve everyone's disposition and good spirits.

'Comparison between ascending politicians and making steel. While you are producing something that is useful cold hard and strong the scum always rises to the top.'

Sir Richard was old school, and his mantra was that you never take the blame for anything that goes wrong, or responsibility for anything that will damage your image. A skilled gentleman politician who had honed and sharpened his skills over many years, I remember he used to delight in putting his underlings (usually some poor university graduate who was working for free to gain experience) in no win situations. Typically, he would be asked to comment on some tricky matter which he would then sidestep by delegating this to the underling, putting them on the spot and forcing them to come up with an answer. He would then congratulate them and shuffle them out of the way somewhere. He, after some deliberation, would then put this solution through if he liked it. If it all worked out, all the praise was his, and if it didn't he had his sacrificial lamb. Well, you have to admire the man.

'Some say he was so crooked that if he swallowed a cat he would shit a rat.'

I remember all the talk at the time was the exit from the **E**xclusive **U**niverse for **R**etiring **O**ld **P**olitico **E**rratic **A**bnormal **N**arcissist (EUROPEAN) union, and how on earth they were going to manage without this marvellous gentleman's club to visit. Still, most of them were not that worried as the UK was stuck in the article 50 catch 22 trap. A masterly piece of legislation some snivelling EU civil servant had dreamed up, and specifically designed to prevent any one country escaping the European Union's insidious bureaucratic clutches, and also ensuring their pointless jobs remain secure. I blame the French.

But I apologise, dear reader, for deviating from my account of the strange and grotesque events leading up to my current predicament. Ah yes... With the local election coming up in a few weeks it was all hands on deck doing canvassing for votes and handing out leaflets to our doting adoring constituents. On one occasion we were canvassing for several tedious hours around the town centre. After an extended period of this, I decided I had enough hand-clasping, flattering, ingratiating and pleasing the voters for the day and proceeded to make my way back home.

For some unknown reason while heading back, some force drew me back to that rather grotty little pub 'Old Victoria Tavern'. It was strange as I don't think I had any urge from my intemperance, but I think it was some greater immoral power that I could not resist and that compelled me to enter. I decided to order a white wine from the bar and took it to a corner table. I presently felt something furry brush against my leg, making me look down. It... it was Gordon. The creature looked up at me with its little black shiny eyes and jumped on to my lap. I hesitantly started to stroke the creature realising now it couldn't be Gordon, remarkably similar though it was. The creature seemed to enjoy being stroked and had soon made itself comfortable. Its presence had a strange almost insidious attraction to me that I can't explain. I slowly started to notice a small but distinct streak of white hair around one eye and down the cheek.

The animal had no collar identification on it, and none of the bar staff or customers claimed the creature as belonging to them.

"Got a new doggie have you love!" one of the locals who was sitting at the bar said loudly. With a beaming grin he laughed. "You want to be careful, maybe it's a baby old black shuck that's found its way here!"

'Old Shuck or old shock was the name given to a large ghostly black dog which it was said roamed the coastline and countryside.'

The creature looked up and gave him a cold stare, which I remember seemed to unnerve him rather and caused the fellow to turn away on his seat. With some awkwardness he crouched over his drink as if to try to diminish his presence. To defuse the sudden tension I replied cheerily and with self-confidence, "It certainly looks that way," adding, "I trust I can rely on your votes for me, Selkie Denison, in the election." This seemed to do the trick and the atmosphere returned to normal.

'In politics the opportunity to make any public relations gain must never intentionally be missed.'

Now, as a dutiful public servant, I know that the Control of Dogs act 1992 requires the dog to have an identifying collar or a microchip tag, and if a person finds a stray dog they must report it to the council dog warden. I decided to take the dog home with me and drop him into the dog warden next time I was passing, or when I went in to work at the council offices.

The dog warden made a note of the dog's details, but as the creature was not tagged and had no other identification, no attempt could be made to find its owner. The warden asked me if I wanted to keep the dog as he was satisfied that I would be a suitable owner, having had experience with looking after animals. So our new Gordon moved in. This animal wasn't to give the happy companionship I thought however.

The Killing of Alex

In the proceeding weeks slowly and almost imperceptibly and for reasons I am at a loss to describe or define, I started to have an increasingly stronger and strange feeling of hatred and ill will towards our new doggy companion. The animal would unfalteringly follow in my footsteps, and wherever I sat it would crouch under my chair, or jump up on my lap and make itself comfortable with its increasingly nauseating presence. This growing dread and horror with which the animal was now inspiring in me, now invoked thoughts of its destruction with a deadly blow or some other savagery, and yet I remember I held back, partly at least by the memory of my former brutality to Gordon, and as such I continued to treat the creature with some level of care.

It was early evening and the daylight was beginning to fade, I remember. I needed to take some items to the cellar for storage and got Alex to help me. The creature as usual was following closely my every move. There were two or three cardboard boxes filled with old bits and pieces, car parts, and a printer I recall. You know we should have really thrown it all away, but you always think something might come in useful so you keep it, don't you.

Alex went down the cellar stairs with the first cardboard box and I followed with another, the creature following close behind. While descending the rather steep stairs the little beast tripped me, almost throwing me forward and headlong to the floor below. Somehow, I managed to get my balance and save myself. Having got to the bottom of the stairs I remember dropping the box, and as my torments mounted, any residue of good within me towards the creature now seemed to succumb to the monstrous thoughts of killing and ridding myself of it.

I saw there was a rather rusty claw hammer among some other tools on the table, and grabbing it took a violent swing at the cursed creature, which of course would have been deadly had it hit its target as I intended. The blow, however, was deflected by Alex grabbing my arm at the last instant and rescuing my pray. Goaded by Alex's unwanted intervention and in a red rage, I withdrew my arm from his holding grasp. I then swung the hammer round to ward him off, but regrettably he just moved too slowly and the claws of the hammer thrust and embedded deep into his throat. His face in shock he opened his mouth slightly, and with barely a groan fell dead on the floor. I do remember looking at Alex's limp body and blood spattered head lying on the cellar floor, and thinking to myself, was it really a homicide or did his actions really just cause his own self destruction.

'Pride causes us to distort the evidence and shift blame to others.'

I looked around the cellar for the small black nemesis, but the hated creature was nowhere to be seen having, I supposed, escaped upstairs and away from my wrathful anger. Seeing I now had to calm down, I set myself the task of concealing Alex's body ensuring at the same time any evidence of his death was eliminated. I thought of cutting the corpse up and disposing of or burying the pieces, but decided that the risk of being observed by neighbours or any passers-by, would be too great. I then hit upon the idea to just pull up some of the floor boards and hide him where the pump house mechanism used to be housed, some fifteen feet or so below the current cellar floor, deep enough for me to entomb and successfully lay to rest any evidence of his presence, at least until it was safe to permanently dispose of him somewhere else.

After some time and persuasion, I managed to remove the floorboards to gain access to the void, and I dragged Alex across the floor and popped him and the murder weapon in. Along with the rusty old horticultural tools, and other items, was a bag of garden lime which I poured down into the void and which settled over the body like a thin white blanket. I would need to get some more to absorb any fluids and odours as the corpse decomposed, but I should be able to obtain this without any suspicions being raised, I thought, and then finish off the concealment by filling up the void with rubble and maybe some dried earth from the garden.

As to any blood spills in the cellar, I carefully scrubbed the floor, and as I had read somewhere blood can leave an iron signature, which forensics tests might find, I filed down some rather large rusty nails I found lying around, into a powder, and scattered this all over the floor after doing my clean up. I also found an old bottle of something called MICR laser printer toner powder, which said contained iron oxide, so I sprinkled some of that on the floor as well. It just goes to show, you never know when some unlikely old rubbish will come in handy.

I had a good look around the house but I had not seen the little black devil since Alex's demise and assumed I had scared it off. I remember I now felt some relief that the cursed creature had finally gone.

To allay any suspicions I rang and let it be known to the staff at the office that the election pressure was making me feel a bit under the weather, so I was just having a few days off. The timing was bad, but as it was early in the campaign it was not essential for me to be present, and they could contact me by phone if required. Over the next couple of days, I purchased the extra lime and finished the concealment of Alex. I needed to get this all completed fairly quickly as Alex would no doubt soon be missed, and people would start to ask awkward questions.

The Police Investigation

It was probably about two weeks or so until suspicions started to be raised about Alex's disappearance, so I decided to report that I had not heard from him for some time and was worried about his whereabouts. In due course, I got a visit from the local constabulary. The doorbell rang about 9:30am and as I approached the front door I could see the outline of two people, one a policewoman in uniform, the other a slightly taller man wearing a khaki mac, I think. I opened the door and the taller figure greeted me.

"Good morning madam, I am DC Liam Marish and the constable here is WPC Lyn Louis. I have been assigned the investigation into your husband's disappearance; so can we come in?"

I opened the door wider and said, "Yes, of course," beckoning them into the lounge.

"Please take a seat D.C. Marish, would you and your constable like a coffee? I was just having one."

I lifted the pot of coffee on the table and proceeded to pour a cup. There were some croissants and cakes on a plate that I moved forward, towards him. "Nutmeg cake?" I said offering him up a piece, which he declined with a hand gesture.

"I would like to ask you a few questions at this stage to help us continue with the investigation," he said, and proceeded to ask his questions and make some brief notes on a small notepad. I quickly evaluated that D.C. Marish fancied himself as a bit of a psychologist and with an air about him that you thought he could identify a lie or erroneous statement 'even' perhaps before it was uttered. I think, however, this was in part due to my own fearfulness and I soon realised he was just going through some standard questions in the forlorn hope of trying to trip me up or get me to incriminate myself in some way. The questioning continued for some time, I remember. I think the detective might actually have believed I was going to confess, at some stage, that I had perhaps caused his disappearance or killed Alex. He was trying to read my mind, to look for any clue I had been lying, but to no avail.

'Political accomplishments for deception and deceit will prove once again assistive in a difficult situation.'

When he had finished running through his question list and scribbling the notes down, he commented that with the evidence he had it couldn't be ruled out that I was involved in Alex's disappearance, but that was fairly routine in these cases.

I at once retorted to this, "What evidence? What evidence can you possibly have to implicate me in this? You must be mad if you think I had anything to do with Alex disappearance."

I even impressed myself at my confident, forceful defence. The thing I quickly learned in politics, (as in life) it is preferable to kick someone while they are down, than to allow them to get up again and force you to fight, and I wasn't going to let this tricky little law man think he had anything on me.

As there was little the police could do at this point, I believe I suggested to the detective that it was time they vacated my house.

Marish then calmly replied, "We will have to do a search of the property." A search of the house, I was told, then they would go and it would be over.

"Fine. Can we get on with it?" I replied confident that they would find nothing incriminating.

The search of the house commenced and of course nothing was found. Then Marish wanted to look around the garden and afterwards the cellar, which he proceeded to do. The garden revealed nothing odd but I noticed he did prod around our little pet cemetery, in one corner, with a long twig he had picked up nearby. He then proceeded back towards the house.

The cellar was the final destination for the search. Upon entering there was a slight but distinctly detectable and repellent smell, like a mixture of onion, sweat and old urine, or as we say in these parts, old piddle.

Fortunately, the smell was not strong but I could see it had got Marish's attention.

Thinking quickly I said, "Oh… sorry about the odour, we have had a problem with rats and I think one's got trapped behind the boiler. Every time we put the heating on, I think its rancid furry little body starts cooking like a rotten sausage down there."

WPC Louis, who was standing in the background, lifted one well-manicured hand to her mouth and grimaced with disgust, but the explanation seemed to satisfy Marish, and after a cursory look around they both left.

After a week or so, however, and with no leads on Alex's whereabouts the police decided they wanted to do another more 'thorough' search of the house, which came as a bit of a shock to me. As luck would have it I did get a small pre-warning of their intentions as they issued an official search warrant. When I was summarily presented with the document, I noticed it contained some clerical errors on it, meaning it could not be served. The slow pace and comparative incompetence of the legal system meant that another warrant would not be issued and presented to me for several days. The smell in the cellar was still evident, although I was sure it was not coming from Alex as the lime, the earth and other rubble he was buried under should have taken care of that. However, as I obviously did not want to raise anyone's suspicions as to the cause, and take the risk it would prompt them to start poking around the cellar too closely, it was time for Bob and Dylan to play their part in the grand deception.

'It was either Bob, Dylan or me, and it wasn't going to be me.'

Having humanely put to death (done in) the white rats, I needed to prepare them for their role, so employing my culinary talents I cooked them in the oven till they were nicely singed and browned. I remember thinking I could have won that 'Celebrity Master Cook' contest they had on the TV, with my baked rodent recipe. Crispy on the outside and soft and succulent in the centre. Suitably prepared, I left them to stand for a while, and then picked them up by their tails and hiding them in the vicinity of the cellar boiler I then sprinkled a few rat droppings around the area.

Betrayal by the Black Nemesis

By the time the police came to do their search of the house, the rats were decaying nicely and starting to give off the desired unpleasant aromatic bouquet, so all was ready for the police to search through my humble little dwelling house.

Several officers came this time, some wearing white coveralls and proceeded to look in every nook and cranny of the property. Having found nothing thus far, the search of the premises moved on and descended to the cellar.

My heart was beating calmly as one who is totally innocent, and with my arms folded across my bosoms I slowly paced the cellar from end to end so as to observe the search unfold. All went according to plan with my well placed rats found and thus successfully explaining the lingering unpleasant cellar smell. With absolutely no traces of blood or other evidence detected, the police were now thoroughly satisfied and prepared to leave. With the search concluded and the party of forensic officers preparing to climb back up the stairs, my victory now seemed assured.

"Well, thank you for your time," I said calmly as they proceeded to ascend, "I am happy your suspicions have now been satisfied. Feel free to call again."

Maybe it was just a little bravado, or perhaps to show-off I stamped my foot down on the very floorboards located above Alex's entombment. It was at this point that the strange abyssal sorcerous events that I can't logically explain, and that ultimately sealed my fate now came to reveal themselves. As the police are my witness, the dark little devil now avenged himself. No sooner had the echo from my foot hitting the floor stopped, than a dull sound like a crying baby or infant came up through the floorboard. The muffled sound gradually becoming louder until it became a high-pitched howling scream. The officers spun around and Marish said there must be a fox or something trapped under the floorboards. Beckoning to some of the other officers he continued, "Quick give me something to help me leaver the floorboards up so we can get it out."

I pondered my stupidity in stamping my foot down, and looking in horror as events unfolded I remember I felt faint as the floorboards came up. Torches were quickly pointed down, lighting up the opening.

"It's too deep, I can't see anything. We will have to get down there and have a look," Marish said. "Quick, help lower me down and give me a torch."

The howling appeared to lessen and then stopped, and within a minute or two the rubble was being moved. A decaying and blood-clotted creature that looked like a small black dog was bought up and placed on the cellar floor. A little dark bloodied glass eye then rolled out ominously from its head onto the floorboards. Somehow, some way as unbelievable as it sounds, I know it was Gordon's rotting corpse, but of course it couldn't be.

Once the creature's body was discovered, unfortunately for me, Alex's blooded and decaying remains were also found and recovered quickly afterwards.

'In every situation there are many factors that can contribute to each outcome but if it is the intended purpose of your dark curse your outcome is set.'

I know that it was really the hideous beast whose sorcery and witchcraft tempted me into murdering, and who's informing, outcrying screeching voice now determined and sealed my fate.

My Incarceration

What my final destiny will be I have yet to discover, as I note I am being observed in my captivity. Still, I know people, important people, so I doubt I will be here for too long, and of course I can console myself with the fact that as a politician I should be able to wiggle and squirm my way out of any situation, 'and' I will get out of this. I must say, however, while I am here they have provided me with a nice cell. All the comforts, and all at the cost of the poor tax payer. Save for the loss of my liberty (and possibly my sanity) I may in fact be doing better than most of our fellow citizens nowadays.

'The black nemesis intent is clear but I have not yet been found guilty of any crime.'

The ghastly image of my mother now appears in front of me, but different from previous incarnations. This time her face had materialised with soft blurred features and misty white in colour, like some disfigured Japanese geisha. "Oh god, not you again mother, that's all I bloody well need!" I said in recognition and without any fear of the phantom now.

43

"Selkie, Selkie, I told you what would happen to you, appreciate that. The inter-temporal smoothing has arrived, your moral traction gone you will now be cast out to a void in space and banished to the depths of Hell."

"Well, thanks very much for that really helpful observation mother dear, it really is bloody nice to see you again too!" I replied sarcastically. "I am not in hell yet you rotten old witch, now why don't you bugger off, go and do some shopping or haunt somewhere else and give me a bit of peace!"

To this the apparition replied, "You always were a rude girl my little Selkie!" With a reddish glow the phantom now slowly dissipates with an indignant outraged look on its face, and lifting its bony finger up in some sort of curious upward demonic pointing signal it disappeared.

If only I had known…

The police report explained the howling screams as probably just due to creaky floorboards and wind, with Gordon's body just a dead creature that I had buried along with Alex. The finding of the body, of course, being masterly detective work on their part. All concocted down the pub no doubt.

**'A policeman once told me don't drink and drive,
it will spill everywhere.'**

Incidentally, I was told that the food inspectors looking into the myristicin poisoning, couldn't find any evidence after extensive testing of the spice cake in the coffee shop, so their investigation was subsequently dropped. I suspect this is just another official cover up.

I think we all must have a little insanity in us, my nemesis realised this and cursed me by finding a way to escape by my intemperance, and released the evil spirit that has cursed me and condemned me to my fate. But, as I said in the beginning, I am Selkie Denison and I am not mad.

It might just be a little crazy but I think it would be a nice gesture if I make a small donation to the RSPCA to help out our little friends and companions, and maybe arrange a lecture with Alcoholics Anonymous.

**'Our sense of worth, of well-being, even our sanity
depends upon our remembering.
But, alas, our sense of worth, our well-being, our
sanity also depend upon our forgetting.'**

– Joyce Appleby

It Really Was Lovely to Meat You

For many thousands of years humans have domesticated the indigenous animals of this planet to help with farming, in warfare, to ride, as companions; 'and as a food source'. However, mankind's assumption that he would remain the unassailable master of this planet and top of the food chain was a fateful and prophetic mistake.

As man reached out further to the stars he, by choice, put into effect a chain of events that turned out to be a catastrophe for mankind. Sending out greetings messages from the long range satellites that were launched, all with specific details about our species and all with helpful directions how to get here and locate us was an error, as it turns out, of apocalyptic stupidity.

Sometime in the near future...

A race far more advanced than our own has come to our planet and defeated our combined military might as easily as the Aztec empire was defeated and destroyed in the 16th century by the superior technology and malevolence of the Spanish army of conquistadors, or how the dictator Napoleon won the battle of Austerlitz in the war of the third coalition in the 19th century.

Defeat is a state of mind. You are defeated only when you accept defeat and assume the hopeless mindset of the defeated person.

– Donald Trump

From the timescale of this account of events Earth had been invaded some 30 years ago and man had been conquered and subjugated by the technologically superior beings called the Asgardons. The new 'masters' of the Earth were of a similar size and body structure to humans and walked on two legs. Their skin was of a light grey-green colour in appearance and very slightly scaly in texture. They had approximately humanoid facial size, with a slightly ridged forehead, short turned up nose and perfectly round ear holes protruding out of the sides of their heads. Another feature was their rather long fleshy tongues, which they would use to occasionally moisten their smooth shiny looking lips, but this appendage did not hinder or slur their speech in any way. Their alien eyes were larger than ours and had rectangular horizontal pupils similar to a goat's eyes in appearance. The pupils giving a sharp panoramic view wider and shallower than would be available with a round or vertical shaped pupil. This allowed them see a wider angle around themselves, and also enhance image quality of objects enabling superior visual acuity.

The Asgardons who settled on Earth adopted a way of life and behaviour that was actually similar to their former and now subjugated human inhabitants.

Although they were perfectly capable of producing replica / synthetic meat variants, most of the Asgardons preferred 'real' farmed meat, and found that after sampling human flesh and meat products they were to their taste, and in addition the metallic quality of the blood was also to their liking. The remaining humans were now reduced to a subclass called manimals and relegated to being selective breeding stock animals, with a few 'breeds' as household pets of their masters.

Dr Clavicep was the Asgardon in charge of the 'Farming and Breeding Livestock Establishment' (FABLE) which had taken over all the responsibilities of the now closed down Breeding Livestock Advancement Department Earth (BLADE). This organisation was now exclusively responsible for selective breeding programmes used to improve and enhance the livestock's ability to produce more and improved cuts of meat and also techniques to slaughter and process the creatures, and had recently been made solely responsible for monitoring all other experimentation on manimals.

From his office Clavicep dialled up on his communication device to contact one of his associates Professor Ergot. The communicator started making a beep, beep, beep high pitched noise. After a brief pause from the device came a reply. "Professor Ergot here, can I help you."

"Ah yes, Dr Clavicep here, I understand you are currently on an educational visit to some of our facilities."

"Yes, that's right, I will be here for about 30 Earth rotations before taking a long journey back to Proxima Centuri and home to Anglanda Prime on the next POLSTAR (Photon-drive Light Speed Transporter) shuttle," Professor Ergot replied.

Clavicep continuing. "I have been asked to front one of those short entertainment education docuprogs on our work here at FABLE, you know the sort of thing… A bit of background into our colonisation and the advancements we are making into our breeding programmes concentrating specifically on our progression with the manimals, that sort of thing. I was wondering if you would help me with overview commentary on this."

"It's a bit of a waste of time I know, but it helps keep the funding coming in. We have actually made some good progress which I think you would be interested in."

"Well, I am quite short on time, but am sure we can sort something out," Ergot replies. "Let me see when I could get over to you and meet you at your office. (Short pause) I can stay for a half Earth rotation. I can get to you, say, Lunar Standard Time about 18:30. You are time zone one so it will be about 18:20. Will that be acceptable?"

Clavicep: "Yes that will be most agreeable, are you sure I can't arrange to get you picked up?"

Ergot: "No, that's fine, it will be quicker and easier for me if I make my own way."

Clavicep: "In that case thank you, and see you then. I will get over a copy of the draft commentary for you to familiarise yourself with before you arrive." Dr Clavicep presses the disconnect on his communicator and scribbles down the meeting time details in his docuprog file notes.

Clavicep wanted to get Ergot to participate, as the Professor had been researching and piecing together some of the culture and background history of the manimals to add to the electronic history database archives upon his return to home planet.

Clavicep had also convincingly pointed out to the producers of the docuprog, that Professor Ergot would be able to check over certain parts of the script where he had an expertise and possibly add some useful comments and observations of his own. So it was quite agreeable to all concerned that Ergot should be invited and encouraged to participate, and of course with Ergot involved this would add extra prestige to the production.

The Docuprog Commentary

Professor Ergot arrives at FABLE and is met by Dr Clavicep. They have a hurried meeting with the docuprog producers to run through and discuss any amendments and final changes to the script. They are then accompanied to a sectioned-off part of the main conference room where their commentary would be added and edited on to the already filmed (docuprog) documentary. Clavicep and Ergot are then ushered to a small desk with high gain speakers attached and both given some headphones to put on.

The production team leader, Synestia comes over to give some preliminary editorial instructions. "Now what we will do is run through the film which you will see in the background in short sections and I will direct you when to read out the various applicable relevant parts of the script. We can then add and edit as required. I will give you any instructions to stop or repeat the commentary over your headphones."

Ergot and Clavicep nod in acknowledgement.

Synestia returns to his control box and after a few moments he is heard to speak though the earphones: "Right, let's get started. Roll film section one... and action."

The initial titles roll and the docuprog begins to play...

Clavicep's and Ergot's commentary begins...

"At the time of our colonisation, we estimate that there were about 9 billion manimals all over the planet, and various other sub groups of creatures."

"From what we know about manimals they generally displayed incredible stupidity, aggression even, against their own kind, and had many other inferior attributes. I think that it is no exaggeration to say that if we had not colonised this planet they would probably have destroyed each other eventually and probably everything else on this planet. It really is stunning that given their low level of intelligence and behavioural traits that they managed to became a dominant species."

"When we arrived at this planet and the manimals became aware of our presence they initially tried to attack us with some primitive radioactive producing projectiles in a futile attempt to stop our colonisation, but of course our deflector and phased weapons easily neutralised and repelled the threat. They did however succeed in irradiating millions of their own species with the fallout that these weapons produced."

"They did have a very primitive communications network, which we think they called the internet, which was easily disrupted and quickly eliminated. With this communication eliminated and ensuring the satellite navigation systems they had were ineffective, we then did away with and rendered useless any other weapon targeting methods they had."

"The next step was for us to send down our robotic, cyber and positronic weapon systems to secure all ground areas before our landing, and the rest, as they say, is history."

"With such an inferior creature as this we could have just eliminated them all like a pestilent disease or other epidemic; but of course that is not the way civilised and compassionate Asgardons behave."

"We here at FABLE are working tirelessly to transform this poor futile creature into a productive source of food and nutrients that all can benefit from, while always keeping its health and well-being as our primary objective."

"We have noticed that manimals are quite prone to skin infection, and we find there is a need to treat symptoms quickly when they become evident. The creatures do also suffer from, and are prone to getting intestinal worms, flea and lice infestations, and there is also a tendency for them to suffer various aliments due to damp and cold weather conditions. Most of this can be fairly easily controlled with the correct animal husbandry techniques we have researched and developed here at FABLE. We like to say at our unassuming little institute here a happy manimal is a productive manimal."

A picture is displayed of a hairy 'manimal' looking in distress with a red identifying tag stapled and inserted through its ear lobe. Held in a constricting restraining cage, it is shown on display with two Asgardon medical technicians dressed in sterile uniforms, checking its teeth and performing various other tests and checks.

"Now it may look like the creature is being subjected to some form of torture but these tight tubular cages are for their own health and well-being. The restrainer cages keep them safe and spare their Asgardon handlers a possible nasty bite or scratch as they give a health check and any other medical treatment or inoculations that may be required."

A second display comes up of an Asgardon technician attempting to insert an oscilloscope type device into the creature via its rectum. The creature is shown struggling in distress and making howling noises as this procedure is being performed. The oscilloscope device is eventually removed and the creature is then seen to quickly calm down.

"As you see, this is a standard anal probe that is being performed on the creature to ensure it is internally free of worms or infection. Incidentally, we did actually adapt this device from one we found that the manimals used on themselves and other indigenous creatures for medical purposes. After some initial trial and error, it has proved very useful for this type of examination. By happy chance, the device can also be used to check down the creature's throat for non-invasive examination into the stomach, and also to take biopsies."

"We at FABLE have recently developed a highly successful anti-clotting additive we call haemophiliac red, so that the nutritious blood can be used as an additive food product that remains easily storable for long periods."

"Also, as part of our ongoing improvement programmes, we are now developing several techniques using drugs and other methods to improve the finished products that you consume. For example we have been running trials using a new selective drug treatment to stop bothersome nail growth. This takes away the need to remove the nails from the digits during their processing (fingers / toes) into what you might recognise as the popular finger licking crunchy dips products."

"Developments in our selective breeding programmes have also produced the large belly manbull and mancow along with other variants."

Several pictures come up on the screen of this speciality breed of manimal and some of the other different experimental breeds.

"The creatures have become much more docile as a result of the breeding programmes, but they do suffer increased mobility and rheumatic problems in their leg joints, due to their increased size and with the speeded up metabolic growth rates we have so far achieved. However, these are quite manageable and are offset by the benefits of significantly increased productivity."

"We are currently doing some long term research into a rather interesting breeding process called parthenogenesis. It is a technique which involves altering the original species so that they will exist in only female form and be able to spawn clones of themselves. This is very experimental at the moment but may possibly yield results in the future."

Ergot and Clavicep's commentary continues in this vain for some time until the end of first section of the docuprog.

The production leader Synestia comes over to speak to them. "Now the commentary has all come through very clearly without problem so far, so thank you. If you would like a short break for refreshments, it will take us a little while before we are ready to proceed with the next section."

Clavicep leans back in his chair pulls down his headphones so that they rest on his shoulders and he stretches his arms forward. Ergot likewise removes his headphones. One of the production assistants then comes over to the desk and asks what refreshments they would each like to have brought over to them, pointing to the buffet that is laid out in the corner of the room.

Clavicep replies, "I will just have a natural aqua, nothing added thank you; what will you have Ergot?"

Ergot replies, "I think I will have an aqua as well but with a shot of some of that treated blood… haemophiliac red. The iron in it helps give my breathing a bit of a boost in this thin atmosphere. Oh and can you slip in a piece of frozen aqua as well please."

"That reminds me I am about due to take my oxygen supplement tablet," Clavicep remarks. He fumbles around in his pocket and sorts out his medication while the assistant goes off to get their drinks.

Ergot sighs and says, "I must say I am looking forward to getting back to home world and breathing some proper air. These off world duties can be very draining."

The atmosphere on 'Anglanda Prime' is a mixture mostly of nitrogen, oxygen and water vapour so is similar to Earth but up to 20% denser due to the planets larger size and proximity to its sun. The planet itself varies at times from being globally slightly dimmer to slightly brighter than Earth due to its elliptical orbit, and its single moon similarly helps regulate Anglanda's tidal movements.

"These manimals of yours, they are not cannibalistic to their young are they?" Ergot enquired to Clavicep.

"No. Curious question; so what made you ask me that?" Clavicep replied.

"Well, I came across some old archive documentation showing some correspondence between

59

the manimals when they could read and write in one of their languages. It had several references to 'a bun in the oven'. Well I think the reference bun is actually son, the term they used for male offspring, and the oven was a sort of primitive cooking device. What I am speculating is that they sometimes used to eat their first born male child in some sort of primitive savage ritual. There are also notes that say 'I am having one in the oven', 'he will be cooked in nine months', 'in the pudding club', 'eating for two' and various other obscure references."

"However, I can't seem to find any other solid evidence to support this theory, so I am not sure if I should include it in the official electronic history database. Any suggestions?"

The young assistant returns with the drinks and places them on table in front them. "Is there anything else I can get you?" she enquires.

"No, thank you," Clavicep replies.

Ergot reaches over and picks up his drink. Taking a sip, he felt it cold and tingly against his neck. The ecstasy as it spilled voluntarily down and down his throat, like a rare pleasure. A second larger sip follows and he then replaces his drink back down on to the table.

Turning to Clavicep he remarks, "This tastes much better than that hydroxyl mix they serve you on long haul shuttles."

Clavicep picks up his drink and takes a large gulp. His drink swallowed and replacing his glass on the table he then replies to Ergots question.

"From my experience manimals usually display a great affection towards their offspring, so I think it highly unlikely they would be naturally cannibalistic. Also, you have to remember they were a species from their leaders downwards, that routinely lied to each other all the time, and who celebrated meanness, aggression and rudeness as desirable traits, which means you need to take this fact into account when that sort of unsupported rather anecdotal information comes up."

"Oh well, it was just that it would have made an interesting footnote in an otherwise rather dull entry on these creatures for my archive report," Ergot replies.

Clavicep: "Well you do actually get some nice succulent carving joints from the baby ones, and I really like a nice tender roast leg of baby in a nice thick meaty gravy juice. I must say that I am not very keen on the side dish pickled eyes though. They are a bit of an acquired taste I think. We commercially produce those here as well, just on a small scale now you know."

The two chat on for a short while and finish their drinks. The production leader, Synestia, comes over and tells Ergot and Clavicep they are now ready to voice over the next section of the docuprog.

They both reposition their headphones, and the producer now back in his sound booth control area asks them through their earphones if they are ready.

Ergot and Clavicep both nod in acknowledgement.

Producer: "Right, let's get started. Roll film section two… and action."

Dr Clavicep begins the commentary…

"The manimals belong to the Eutheria which is a subclass of mammals native to this planet all of which have a placenta and reach a fairly advanced state of development before birth. From what we know this group includes most mammals on this planet with a few exceptions."

Several pictures come up on the screen showing depictions of female manimals and other mammals, in various stages of pregnancy, with timescale data also presented.

An alarm on Clavicep's communicator suddenly starts to ring along with a small flashing signal light. Over their headphones can be heard Synestia loudly saying 'cut' and the film is abruptly halted.

"Oh, I am sorry we have a security problem, you will have to excuse me for a moment," Clavicep says.

Getting up he quickly takes off his earphones and rapidly makes his exit to a nearby hallway to take the call away from the others.

He clicks on his communicator receiver. "Hello, Clavicep here, what's the problem?"

"Sargon here…"

Sargon is head of the institute's security. A rather cold blooded individual with a dominant manor, and who if angered would have revenge both cruel and subtle on his unfortunate victim.

"One of the manimals appears to have made its escape from temporary experimental area at building 101 while some tests were being carried out. I have put into effect the standard escape protocol and obviously if the manimal does manage to get over the outer security barrier wall, it will be killed immediately to avoid any threat."

Clavicep: "Listen Sargon, I want to avoid killing or injuring the creature if possible, it could be a valuable experimental animal. Get me the details of how it escaped and deploy some of the observation security drones to search for it. Just arm them with HV plasma inverter weapons for now. A blast from one of those should effectively shock its nervous system and disable it ready for you to capture. I will leave you to contain the problem but keep me informed, and try to avoid doing anything that will alarm our visitors, the last thing we need is any bad publicity."

Sargon: "Of course; leave it with me Dr Clavicep. I will contact you when we have more information. It shouldn't take me long to recapture the beast."

Clavicep turns off his communicator and returns to the main conference room. Synestia comes over to him. "Is there a problem doctor?"

Clavicep: "We have had a very minor safety breach with one of our manimals at the experimental laboratory, but our security team are sorting it out now so nothing to worry about. 'But…' I may possibly get called away again as the creature may need my attention. Unfortunately these things happen, but we have no problem proceeding with the commentary at present."

Synestia: "Fine, fine, if you get back in position and replace the headset we will carry on."

Ergot and Clavicep's commentary continues without further interruption until the end of the next section of the docuprog and Synestia is heard to say, 'cut' and congratulate everyone on successful completion of that part of the docuprog.

With another small interlude until commencement of the final section of the docuprog commentary, and as Clavicep had not heard anything from Sargon, he decided to contact him and get an update on the escaped manimal.

Casually remarking to Professor Ergot that he needed to make a call and would be back shortly he removed his earphones made his way to the nearby corridor again.

Through a large window he can see it is overcast and raining quite heavily with small streaks of water running down the glass. A low rumbling thunderclap can be heard in the distance. Clavicep turns on his communicator to contact Sargon. It takes a few seconds to connect and for Sargon to answer.

"Yes, Doctor, I was just about to contact you. You will be glad to know that we have now caught the brute, but unfortunately it did sustain a few minor bangs and bruises. I have arranged for it to be taken back to building 101 where it escaped from and be placed in one of the secure holding pens. I still need to interview the technicians on duty to confirm exactly how it managed to escape but I will give you a full report in due course. I assume that is satisfactory."

Knowing Sargon's cruel streak, Clavicep asks how the creature got injured.

Sargon replied that the drones had it cornered by one of the outer buildings, and they surrounded it ready for capture. Although the beast looked exhausted by this time and was on its knees trying to crouch by the wall, when they approached it, it staggered up from this position and then onto its feet, laughing and chuckling all of the time, it was evidently crazy or mad with anger. The beast then came at them with a large rock in its hand.

Sargon: "Nearer two or maybe three paces and then… then it slipped on the wet ground and fell face downward on the soaked grass where we grappled with it and managed to put on the restraining cuffs and a head guard. The manimal got its injuries in the struggle to capture and subdue it. Couldn't be avoided I am afraid."

Clavicep didn't entirely believe Sargon's explanation, but it was only a manimal after all, and it had been successfully recaptured.

"Get the technicians to look after the creature and tell them I will get over there to check on things when I have finished here."

Sargon: "Very good doctor."

Clavicep disconnects the call and returns to the conference room. After making small talk with Ergot for a short period of time, they are informed that everything is ready to complete the final section of the docuprog voice-over.

Producer: "Right now... Roll film section three... and action."

Professor Ergot begins the commentary...

"To complete the manimal's life cycle as a domesticated food source, we will look at the slaughter process and where the various prime and other cuts are taken as it is processed and prepared ready for consumption."

An image comes up of a manimal being led into a white tiled room and strapped to a metal chair. Entering the room to the rear of the restraining chair an Asgardon worker picked up a large sharp knife from a tray placed on a nearby table, and from behind with a quick slashing movement cuts the creature's carotid artery. The creature could be heard making a sort of gurgling drowning sound as the darkest, red-coloured blood comes squirting and sputtering out of its neck, making a shiny pool around the body. After several seconds of involuntary movement the body becomes lifeless.

"Directly cutting the throat is basically how we used to slaughter our creatures. An alternative method was to have a chest spike inserted close to the creature's heart, but in both these methods the main vein or artery is severed."

A second image showing a still picture of a manimal having a chest spike inserted comes up on the screen.

"We believe now that this could be unnecessarily painful and possibly cruel to the creatures, so to ensure a rapid death with a minimum of suffering, currently we stun them just before slaughter. We have also improved the way processing is carried out with the introduction of much more mechanised methods of production."

A mechanised manimal meat processing plant is shown in operation with the creatures being led in. They are shackled by their waists and arms and attached to conveyor belts. They are slowly turned upside down and their heads are dipped in liquid with an electric current passing through it. The creatures can be seen to shake as they are stunned, and the machinery moves on to the next stage of cutting their throats and collecting the drained blood for processing.

"Unfortunately, at present a few manimals may not be stunned adequately with this system. Perhaps the manimal moves and misses the liquid stunner bath, or sometimes the electrical current used may be insufficient."

"We have been working on an alternative method here at FABLE where the creatures are stunned with a gas, which can be more effective."

"The actual slaughter method involves some initial cutting, opening up of the major body cavities and the removal of the innards comprising of entrails and organs, but usually leaving the carcass initially in one piece. Later, the manslayer (butcher) will process the carcass into smaller cuts."

A two-dimensional black image is shown on the screen with a patchwork of white lines displayed on it, showing where the various cuts of meat came from on the manimal. Further images follow of the processed meat all packed and ready to leave the factory.

"Of course, nowadays we make use of and process the blood and other nutritious parts in food preparation that we have not traditionally used. Any material that is not used is processed into a protein animal feed or fertiliser."

More examples of products and processes are explained by Ergot and Clavicep, with various pictures showing these until the end of the final section of the docuprog is completed. The closing credits come up on the screen and after a few more seconds it goes blank.

Ergot and Clavicep remove their headsets.

Synestia, the producer, comes over. "Dr Clavicep, Professor Ergot that was marvellous; we can get it all wrapped up now and get out of your way. The studio will be in touch with you in due course Dr Clavicep."

Synestia pats Clavicep on the shoulder as he gets up from his seat. Synestia picks up some papers from the desk and turns to walk away as Ergot looks at his timepiece.

Ergot says to Clavicep: "It is about 5:30 Lunar Standard Time and I need to catch my shuttle back by about 6:30, so I think I had better make arrangements to get there. Don't want to miss my connection!"

Synestia stops and replies, "Well, we should be all packed up well before then. Our transport has plenty of room so please allow me to give you a lift to the shuttle departure area."

Ergot: "That is most considerate of you, I will take you up on your offer. Thank you."

"Think nothing of it professor, a pleasure."

Clavicep: "Well, I need to check on one of my manimals anyway. Professor would you like to come along while we have some time to spare?"

Ergot: "Yes, thank you, I would be most interested in seeing some of the facility."

Clavicep: "Synestia, if you can let me know when you will be ready to leave I will arrange to get the professor back here to you. You have my communicator code."

Synestia nods in agreement of the arrangement and Clavicep ushers Ergot in the direction of the experimental block housing room, 101.

Tour of Room 101

Within a few minutes Clavicep and Ergot had reached Room 101. Clavicep enters a security code and opens the door. The room itself is sub-divided into several areas with a large space containing various laboratory worktops and apparatus. To the middle of the room, and sectioned off by glass screens, were the surgical operating and dissecting tables and to the rear of these were several animal holding pens.

There were three or four Asgardons performing various tasks and Clavicep looked around and recognised Orrin, a female technician looking at some microscope slides. He called to her. Orrin looked up and removing her safety spectacles got up and approached them.

Clavicep: "Orrin, this is Professor Ergot. He has been kindly helping with the docuprog and I thought I would give him a quick tour of some of the facility, before he heads off back to home world."

Orrin nods at Ergot in greeting. "It is a pleasure to meet you professor, I hope you find your tour interesting."

Ergot: "I am sure I will."

Orrin: "Let me show you around the experimental unit."

Orrin proceeds to walk them round some of the apparatus, pointing out features and applications. She picked up a device the size of a small book with a display screen on it and called this a MOMIS (Mobile Multi Image Scanner). Orrin started pointing to parts of the machine developed at FABLE and started to explain what it did. "This has multiple medical uses with an array of sensors in a mobile internal scanner recorder. Very useful for easily checking for internal injury or to analyse skin infections, malignant growths that sort of thing."

Orrin puts the device in her pocket and they proceed with the tour through to the surgical operating area, and finally to the holding pens at the rear and an outside sizeable fenced yard, where the creatures could be allowed to move about freely.

In one of the pens was a rather large pig-like creature resting on the floor. It was covered with loose folds of pink skin which was liberally freckled with light brown spots.

"Ah, here is Ramsay, one of our test animals," Orrin remarks, and she strokes and pats the creature kindly on the head before moving on to the next pen.

Looking into the next pen and seeing the manimal wrapped in a blanket with its back to them and making jerky movements, Ergot remarked, "Your manimal here looks like he is shivering with cold."

Orrin replies, "Oh, you mean the jitters. Unfortunately, for reasons we don't yet fully understand, a prion protein is destroying its brain cells. One of the early symptoms is the involuntary muscle movements you can see."

Clavicep: "This disease also leads to confusion, difficulty walking and ultimately death. We seem to be getting more and more cases showing up. I tell you Ergot, I am worried about this."

As they are speaking, the creature turns round revealing a large area of blue bruising around its bloodied left eye and jaw. One hand is also bound with a bandage.

Clavicep: "Is this the manimal that escaped?"

Orrin: "Yes, Doctor. He was in quite bad shape when Sargon's operatives brought him back."

She takes out her mobile medical scanner and directs it to the manimal to show Ergot its function.

Clavicep: "Sargon said the creature picked up a rock and attacked them."

Orrin: "The brain disease is causing the poor creature to have difficulty walking, and I doubt if it could hold a rock let alone attack them. In any case, manimals are not aggressive anymore. The disease only seems to affect the older manimals at the moment, so we may need to slaughter them earlier to eliminate the problem. The brain and spinal cord are removed and not used in their processing, so there is no danger of any cross contamination to Asgardons from our meat products."

Clavicep: "We originally thought that he increased prevalence of the disease was being caused by the growth hormone or certain transplanted human tissues, but have assessed this risk as insignificant as we have improved our sterilisation techniques, and now use synthetic sources of the hormone. Actually, we think the cause of the increase in cases is likely due to their feed, as this contains waste processed protein from various animal brain parts and bones."

Orrin: "Recently, to make the cost of processing their protein feed biscuits cheaper, some of the microbe disinfection procedures when reviewed were relaxed, and some stopped entirely."

Clavicep quietly observed the manimal. "Orrin, arrange to draw off some cerebrospinal fluid from its spinal cord to test now, along with an electroencephalogram readout of the brain's pattern of electrical activity. When the disease has progressed to serious confusion, inability to walk and mood changes, we will remove the brain and see what that reveals."

Orrin: "Yes Doctor, I will schedule in the procedures."

Orrin takes a few sweets from her pocket and gestures the manimal to come towards her. The creature shuffles over, and holding out its shaking hand takes them from her. It turns and moves slowly back to the corner of the pen.

Clavicep's communicator activates and he answers.

Synestia: "Hello Doctor, we are just about ready to leave now if you can get the professor back to the conference room."

Clavicep: "Fine, we will be back with you shortly."

Clavicep deactivates his communicator and replaces it back in his pocket.

"Well, Ergot, looks like this is the end of the tour. What do you think of our little facility?"

Ergot: "It is certainly impressive, what you have achieved so far. I was wondering though, you said your manimal managed to escape from here, how did it do that?"

Orrin: "Oh, I can answer that if I may. We were remotely monitoring the manimals agitation, involuntary muscle movements and difficulty walking in the secure compound at the rear of the pens. Some of the building materials being stored ready for the building extension collapsed on to the fencing, and created a small gap. By the time someone noticed what had happened, our stealthy little manimal had slipped out."

"Mind you, after Sargon had finished with him, I think he wished he hadn't."

Clavicep: "Come on Ergot, I have got to get you back for your lift. Orrin, thank you for showing us around."

Ergot: "Yes, thank you so much."

Clavicep leads Ergot back to the conference room, and thanking him for his help with the docuprog sees him off.

Just another day concludes at the FABLE research and manimal food production facility on Earth.

> *Treat your inferior as you would wish your superior to treat you.*
>
> — *Seneca the Younger*

Molary

Now dentists have always made me uneasy, it's not that dentists are bad people, and to be certain, quality dental care is an essential necessity to your general health. If you don't get those six monthly check-ups, your teeth could literally fall out of your mouth. Also most dentists, I am sure, primarily must do their job because they enjoy a mixture of helping their patients, the reasonable office hours and, of course, the highly generous salary that goes with it all, 'and' unlike in the good old days when they were expected to do everything themselves, many now have their underlings the wretched Hygienists to do the menial tasks. This, of course, inevitably adds another layer of charges to their bills. No wonder you never seem to see a miserable tooth doctor. Dentistry, it seems to me at any rate, to be the one area of medicine that seems to hark back to the dark ages where agony and torture were a harmful, injury causing, commonplace part of 'the treatment'. So while the other branches of our health care have grown in sophistication and expertise in their execution, dentistry hasn't really developed beyond refinements on and variations in cleaning, drilling, and yanking out our troublesome teeth with a big shiny pair of pliers. Yes, granted without doubt there have been important advances made in the field, but any such progress is undermined by the horrific stories of things that can and do happen in the dentist's chair. My name is Warwick Charas and this is one such story.

It begins with the reason for my unavoidable visit to my dentist, Dr Hesaltine. Unsurprisingly, I had a toothache. It was the familiar type of recurrent toothache which had been giving me pain, off and on, for a while. For no obvious reason this had rapidly got much worse over the course of the day. I remember that the effect was now giving me a highly agonising extreme sensory pain that felt like it was pressing on, and coursing, through my tooth, and in addition to this I could feel it starting to create a swelling pressure area on my face.

With the pain now shifting all other thoughts and feelings aside, I resolved that I could put it off no longer, and ringing up the surgery I managed to organise a hurried appointment for 4.30pm the next day.

I actually had quite a good night's sleep, probably as a result of the paracetamol and a couple of shots of whisky I had taken before bed. By the next morning the pain had thankfully eased significantly and alleviated my suffering. I knew this couldn't last, but was grateful to have some reprieve from the pain. Teeth seem to be perfectly designed to specifically only feel pain, there seems to be no other toothy feelings I can think of. If a nerve happens to be even slightly exposed and unprotected in there, it's 'all' pain. Cold is 'all' pain, warm is 'all' pain, touch is pain, even a bit of wet saliva seems to bring on the pain. Well you get the idea, there is very little worse, let's face it, than a nice severe tooth ache.

I arrived at the dental surgery a few minutes early, parked the car, and proceeded into the building through a pair of white painted and glazed entrance doors. Directly in front was the reception counter, and emblazoned on it a large backlit toothbrush symbol with the dental surgery name printed below in bright lilac-coloured letters. I proceeded to book in with the help of the rather attractive and young looking brunette on the other side. Immaculately dressed in her white clinical uniform, she proceeded to type in my details on to her computer terminal, and with this done I was directed to the waiting area. I always think it is a bit strange why the reception staff dress up so they look like they are the clinical workers. I imagine it is supposed to convey some sort of calming psychological effect of efficiency and confidence for the hapless victim.

After sitting in the waiting area for what seemed like only a couple of minutes, I was ushered into Dr Hesaltine's treatment room by his rather plump, but nonetheless attractive, dental nurse assistant who displayed a beaming smile that revealed her perfectly straight white teeth. She directed me to, and parked me into, the dreaded dentist chair from where there was no escape.

Having briefly glanced at my medical notes, Dr Hesaltine, a tall individual with greying locks of hair protruding from each side of his balding head like some eccentric professor, then came over and greeted me.

"Hello Warwick, open up and we will have a look around and see what the problem is," he said, with lips curled up in a reassuring grin. I leaned back on the chair headrest and opened my mouth.

"Open wider," he requested, which I did. Halting for a moment, he then proceeded with his examination.

"Upper Right 1, 2, 3, 4, 5, 6, 7, 8. Upper Left 1, 2, 3, 4, 5, amalgam filling. May need to crown this one at some stage, 6, 7, 8. Lower Right 1, 2, 3, 4, 5… Hmm, here we are, molar number 6. Nurse, large cavity in LR6." He then proceeded to give it a prod with his scraper tool.

I had an immediate sensation of excruciating agony. In response I pressed back in the dentist chair, my hands gripping the arm rests so that my knuckles began to go white.

"My God!" he said startled. "You've got the biggest cavity I've ever seen – the… biggest cavity I've ever seen."

"Look Doctor!!" I replied. "I'm scared enough without you hurting me and then repeating I have a hole in my tooth!"

"I didn't!" he replied. "That was the echo." And laughing he continued, "Relax my boy, it was just a little dentist joke."

"Right, you haven't had an x-ray for a while so we will get one done to check that there is no periapical abscess, as the decay looks quite advanced, then we will see about getting you booked in for treatment."

"Nurse, can we get the x-ray done now," he said. The nurse moved and arranged the x-ray machine to the correct position with some direction from Dr Hesaltine.

"Open wide," he said to me and slipped the x-ray shield into my mouth (which made me feel like choking). "Bite down and hold still," he instructed as they left the room. X-ray taken and within a few seconds they were back. The x-ray shield now with a small coating of saliva on it was swiftly removed from my mouth.

"Alright?" he enquired. I nodded. "Right, just wait a few minutes while we process the x-ray and I can have a look at it."

While we were waiting, he told me a story about his father.

"My dad; Dicky, I think you might know him, came in for dental treatment last week," he said. "He is getting on a bit and has generalised advanced periodontal bone loss. Anyway, I told him to relax in the chair while I went off to see another patient. I asked our new hygienist Lyndsay to obtain a maxillary preliminary alginate impression. She was quite keen to do it and get some experience dealing with the patients, and I thought, what can go wrong."

"Well when she went in to do it, he had semi-dosed off and so she just proceeded to put the alginate putty in. She then removed the impression from Dicky's mouth, and left it on the bench." (He tapped on the desk area to indicate where it had been left.) "When I came back and had a look in his mouth, I realised 'both' maxillary central incisors were missing." (He pointed to the top front teeth of his mouth to indicate to me which ones.) "I quickly checked the impression, and to my absolute horror what do I find, there they were, Dicky's two maxillary central incisors sitting large as life in the alginate impression staring back at me! Mind you, just as well it happened to him, as I don't think he even noticed he had lost them. I ended up having to put a temporary bridge in for him. Funny," he paused. "Dicky looked a bit like an indigent squirrel with the shiny white replacements in his mouth."

I nodded tentatively as he was telling me this, not sure if it was just a fabricated story, one of his jokes or god forbid, it was 'actually' true.

He continued in a more pessimistic tone, "Occasionally, you expect the hygienist might pull out the odd loose filling which needs replacing, but not her. She is fully trained up you know, not a trainee or anything! Only been here for about a month, and well qualified with all her certificates and diplomas and so on, so you would think she would be capable. You just can't sack them nowadays otherwise you get sued. I just don't know."

The door swung open and his plump dental assistant nurse came back in with the x-ray image and handed it over. Dr Hesaltine inserted it in the scanner and within a second or two was looking at an enlarged image through the monitor and pointing out something to the nurse, to which she nodded attentively.

Turning round to me he said, "Right, we have got a bit of a problem, the tooth is badly infected so we can either try root canal, which I don't think will work, or I can just pull it, and clean out the infection, which should sort it."

"I will do what you think best," I said.

"Right," he said rather gleefully, "I will arrange for you to get some antibiotics for the infection and you can book in an appointment. I will sort out that troublesome little bugger for you, and whip it straight out. You will be back to normal in no time."

With that I was ushered out into the reception area to wait my turn to pay for my treatment, plus prescription and arrange the next appointment. I was told I would have to wait ten days before I could get my appointment for the extraction, so needed a prescription note to cover this period of time, and was also advised to gargle with mouthwash or salt water morning and evening.

While they were preparing my bill and prescription, I went and sat down in the reception area. A couple of ladies were also waiting when I took my seat. One was sitting on a chair in the corner. She had a rather oval shaped face and mousy shoulder length hair and had on one of those fluffy looking pink mohair jumpers. She occasionally bit her fingernail and she looked tense and worried. Her skin, I noticed, had a sallow yellowish tint to it, which made it somehow look more apparent to me she was in some distress. From my observation and having (as I considered) an extensive knowledge on the subject, I reasoned and considered that she was clearly a 'dentophobic'. Old Hesaltine's going to have his hands full pacifying and calming that one down I thought to myself.

The other woman was on the other side to me and calmly sitting cross-legged on her seat by the magazine rack, thumbing through a glossy publication. Now she was wearing a short expensive looking fur coat and underneath a revealing white scoop-neck blouse, had black patent boots over her tight skinny black jeans, and a shiny black belt with a large flashy silver buckle round her waist. She was fairly short, petite you might say, although when she stood up to replace the magazine her high heeled boots effectively disguised any lack of stature. I would guess she was in her early 50's but her precise make-up and her full silky red lips made her look much younger. She had lustrous, curly jet black hair with only a few wisps of grey beginning to show here and there. I did notice that she was not wearing any jewellery or rings, apart from two small expensive looking diamond encrusted heart shaped studs in her ears, which for some reason seemed to be rather odd to me considering her other attire.

Dr Hesaltine's nurse assistant came back to pick up some dental records from the receptionist. Turning round to face the reception seating area, and looking at the nervous woman, she said loudly. "Mrs Kendrick! Doctor is ready to see you now."

She paused for a moment to check the notes. "Have you taken your two 5mg Valium tablets Trudy?"

The anxious woman who was sitting in the corner now nodded her head in response. She gets up and is ushered in to Dr Hesaltine's surgery treatment room.

The receptionist then called out 'Ms Curry' to come over and our voluptuous raven-haired lady put her magazine down and walked over to the counter, her high heels clicking on the floor. I had seen her before at the dentists, though I doubt she noticed me. I think she was a regular for one of their special 'film-star' whitening treatments to keep the old grin looking like a well-polished set of pearls.

Within a few seconds, I was also called over by the receptionist to make my payment. Now Ms Curry had picked up one of those miniature toothpaste samples and was opening it, presumably to sniff or taste the contents while she was waiting for the receptionist to print out her receipt. I, meanwhile, was fumbling in my back-pocket to get my wallet out.

Suddenly, there was an almighty scream from old Hesaltine's treatment room. Ms Curry, startled by the noise squashed the paste tube and a pellet of paste shot out at a perfect trajectory to hit me right on the crutch of my dark trousers.

"It's alright, don't panic everybody," the receptionist said as she returned with the receipt. "Mrs Kendrick is always a bit nervous at the dentist's." She hands over the receipt to Ms Curry.

Ms Curry confusingly retorted, "But that was a man's scream."

"Yes, you would have thought his reflexes would have improved a bit by now," the receptionist replied.

Turning around to me I could see Ms Curry's eyes now slowly tracking down to the white blob on my trousers. With the receptionist now also looking at the amorphous blob, I quickly grabbed some tissues that were on the counter and frantically tried to rub it off. Unfortunately, the more I rubbed the more the stain spread out until it had become several times larger than the original spot of paste.

"That will be the titanium dioxide. They put that in to make the toothpaste look nice and white. You won't get that off by rubbing it," the receptionist then rather unhelpfully commented.

"Oh, I am soo sorry," Ms Curry said. "Let me pay for cleaning them."

"No, that is quite alright," I replied, "I will just wash it out when I get back home."

"Look, if you won't accept any money let me give you something," she said, and rapidly sorted through her purse, her slender bright red nailed fingers pulling out a business card. She handed it to me. "That's my company... Cynthia C Apparel," she said with some pride. "You might see something you like on the web site. Let me know, and it's yours."

We heard a car tooting a couple of times outside and she quickly turned round grabbed open one of the glazed entrance doors and yelled out, "Coming JP."

Turning round to me again she said, "Must rush darhling, my lift has arrived. I am so, so sorry about your trousers and I am sure you will be able to get the stain out." And with that, she quickly headed out of the double doors and was gone.

A few more muffled sounds and the odd angry swear word could still occasionally be heard coming from old Hesaltine's surgery room, but no more screams. Can't be much wrong with her teeth if she can inflict that kind of pain, I remember thinking.

The receptionist took my money and gave me my prescription for the pain killers, plus a small card with the next appointment time and date on it.

I decided to pick up the prescription straight away and then get back home, as my tooth was beginning to throb a bit.

I parked the car outside Patel's Pharmacy and went in.

"Hello Mrs Patel, how are you today?" I enquired as I approached the pharmacist standing behind the counter.

"Hello Warwick. I am most agreeable thank you, and how are you?"

She looked down and her eyes widened; the stain on my trousers had been spotted. "Yuck, what happened to you…" she distastefully remarked. "Got pooped on by one of the pidgins did you, or is it something else?"

"Oh! No, no… It's only toothpaste," I quickly and rather embarrassingly replied. "I had an accident at the dentists and the stain won't come out."

I handed over my prescription to her.

"And how is Mr Patel?" I asked in an attempt to divert her attention.

"Oh, the old fool is just the same." She sighed deeply. "Fit as a fiddle and totally bloody useless."

"I am allergic to Penicillin. Can you make sure the medication the dentist has given me will be OK?" I said, as I had forgotten to check this when they issued the prescription.

Looking at the prescription she replied, "Oh, let me see… Erythromycin, that is perfectly fine as a Penicillin substitute. You just need to take one twice a day after meals."

"Give me a few minutes to get this ready," she remarked. "That stain doesn't look very sanitary, we have some stain remover you might want try over there." She pointed to a shelf before turning round and disappearing to the drug dispensing room at the back.

I found the stain remover product, which looked just like a bar of soap. Picking this up, I wandered back to the counter and handed it over to Mrs Patel when she came back with my prescription.

"Give it a good rub in and that will shift it," she assured me. I thanked her and leaving the store with my purchases went back to my car and headed home.

***

The ten days passed relatively quickly even though I was in some pain. No doubt because, believe it or not, I wasn't relishing the prospect of old Hesaltine ripping my molar out.

I made it to the dentists about ten minutes early and this allowed me sufficient time to get the car parked and arrive in a nice calm state ready for the undertaking I was about to endure. Opening one of the glazed double doors, I entered into the building and approached the counter. I duly booked in with the same young brunette receptionist who was there on my last visit.

"Take a seat Mr Charas," she said, "I do apologise but Dr Hesaltine is running a bit late. Hopefully, you won't have to wait too long."

I took my seat in the waiting room, now having been given slightly longer to contemplate my fate.

I looked over at the magazine rack but decided I didn't really want to read anything and so just sat there and aimlessly stared around the room.

The entrance door opened and in came a tall man with well-tanned skin that displayed a golden brown tint. He had a thin face, pork chop sideburns and a moustache that was curled up slightly at the ends. This made him look somewhat wizard like, although I got the impression he thought he looked very suave and sophisticated.

He approached the counter. "Hello darling; Jason P. Wynguard, but you can call me JP," he said to the receptionist. "I have an appointment with your lovely new hygienist hotty. Old Cynth thinks I have got bad breath and need to get it sorted out."

The receptionist typed in the details. "Ah yes Mr Wyn… er JP, you are all booked in now to see Lyndsay. Please take a seat and she will see you shortly."

He came over and sat a couple of seats away from me. Curiosity now got the better of me and I had to ask. "Hello," I said, "Sorry, I don't mean to sound nosey, but was it you who picked up Ms Curry from here last week?"

"Oh, you know Cynthia," he replied, "Yes, that was me, as she who must be obeyed, beckoned call."

We chatted for a short while and it turns out Cynthia Curry used to be a prominent politician until something was leaked to a national newspaper about a policy scandal involving some Arabs, prostitutes and a corrupt bribing scandal that would lead to the loss of a substantial amount of taxpayers money and also some jobs. There was subsequently a big public inquiry and she had to resign. She has done alright since though, as she set up this online company selling her own brand 'Cynthia C' expensive sexy underwear and clothing. She does very well out of this apparently, as a lot of her customers are from the House of Lords.

I said to him that his halitosis problem, which I hadn't really noticed, might just be due to dehydration, as I remember having read this somewhere, but he just laughed and assured me he drank like a fish.

He got called into the Hygienist's, and soon after Dr Hesaltine's dental nurse came for me. Directing down on to the dreaded dental chair she then walked behind me and started preparing the equipment.

"Are you feeling alright, Warwick?" Old Hesaltine now enquired.

A bloody sight better than I am going to feel in a few minutes I thought to myself, but nonetheless replied, "Good, thank you, doctor."

"Great, let's get on with it then shall we; open wide." After prodding around the gum of the bad molar with his gloved finger and then a scraper tool, he remarked that the antibiotics seemed to have worked well eliminating any infection.

He wedged some cotton rolls in the right side of my mouth, and after removing these swabbed around the area with a numbing gel. Next, the large metal syringe went in and I felt a dull pressure on my gum as he started pumping the anaesthetic into the tissue. Then I felt that horrible painful stinging sensation as it worked its way in.

He pulled the syringe out and left me for a few seconds while he unwrapped a pair of pliers and checked he had some swabs to soak up the blood.

After clamping the pliers in place, he started yanking and pulling them back and forth, and at the same time I could hear the molar cracking and crunching. At least the anaesthetic was doing its job, and eventually he managed to pull part of the tooth. Out it came, white at the top and bloodied and browny-red at the root. He held the molar up in front of me triumphantly, clamped between the pliers. The rest of the tooth came out relatively easily now, and he inserted a swab dressing over the hole. "Bite down," he told me, and walked off somewhere for a few minutes as I sat with blood slowly soaking into the dressing, while I recovered a bit.

Coming back and looking down at me he removed the swab and warned, "The anaesthesia will last several hours. You may find it difficult to speak clearly and eat or drink. Be careful not to bite down on the numbed area or you could hurt yourself." I dribbly thanked him and staggered my way out of his treatment room.

Before leaving the surgery, I had to make a payment at reception for the treatment, and arrange a follow on appointment. The dental nurse said she would also sort out a few extra swab dressings for me to take home in case the gum started bleeding again. While this was being sorted out, I just sat down in the waiting area and tried to recover a bit.

Although I was rather groggy, I remember hearing one of the staff speaking nervously on the reception phone to someone. I think she mentioned the names Mr Wynguard, Lindsay and something about tooth or filling replacements, but as my mind was in a state of lethargy still, I wasn't really paying that much attention.

I, after a while, felt slightly better but didn't feel up to driving back home, so arranged to get picked up, agreeing with them I could leave my car overnight in their car park and collect it the next day. As the following day was Saturday, the receptionist advised me the surgery and car park area would only be open until 12.00 noon, and then closed all day Sunday.

***

On the Saturday morning I had recovered my senses and was feeling better, although my gum was still very tender and a bit swollen. I moved my tongue around the wound probing the empty void that used to be my tooth. There seemed to be something slightly jagged that I could feel in the gum, and I thought that maybe I would ask them to check this for me.

Preparing some tepid salty water in a glass, I gave my mouth a good rinse out, got dressed and was ready to retrieve my car. I decided to go by bus down to the surgery as there was a bus stop within about 5-10 minutes walking distance of it. It was about 9.30am so I headed off to my bus stop, got boarded on the bus and then off again at the stop near the surgery by 10am.

After a brisk walk, I arrived at the surgery and went round to the car park area. I was just going to get it and drive back home, but rubbing my tongue over the gum I decided I would try and see if there was someone who could check it was all alright while I was here.

I went in the surgery, but there was no one at reception and no patients waiting to be seen, which was odd. I decided to wait for the receptionist to come back and after a few seconds a rounded but rather thin-faced woman, with a slightly freckled creamy complexion and a frowning displeased expression on her lips, came over to where I was standing. She was wearing white medical overalls and had hanging under her chin around her neck a surgical mask. She was also wearing one of those medical headscarf's holding in her luxuriant blonde hair.

"I am sorry, we are closed today. Water leak. Didn't you see the closed sign?" she said quickly and rather abruptly as though she had been caught off guard.

"I didn't see any sign outside and the entrance doors were not locked," I said, "Have a look for yourself if you don't believe me."

She went quickly to the entrance doors, partly opened one, and sticking her head out had a quick look around and shut the door again. Locking the doors by pushing the floor bolt down. She then turned round to face me. "Must have blown down," she grumbled.

I do recall hearing the occasional dull muffled banging racket coming from somewhere, but didn't really think anything of it. I suppose I thought it was something to do with the plumbing problem.

I explained to her that I had my tooth pulled the day before and was aware of something that didn't feel quite right in the gum. I then asked her if old Hesaltine would have a quick look at it while I was here.

"No, the doctor is not available to see you now!" she said abruptly. "But I can give you a quick look over."

"Oh. Who are you?" I asked hesitantly.

"I am the head hygienist here, Lyndsay, Lyndsay Agnosia. I am fully qualified, registered with the GDC

(General Dental Council) and have a Diploma in Dental Hygiene from the University of Bristol."

It's funny, but I began to feel decidedly uneasy, and my thoughts were just to get out and back to the safety of my car and then back home. "That's very, err, kind of you," I replied awkwardly to her offer, "but I think I would rather wait until I can see Dr Hesaltine. Perhaps next week I can ring in for an appointment."

Now, usually I try to keep my distance from hygienists if I possibly can. To quote them: 'It is very unlikely that a dental hygienist will cause any damage to the teeth and surrounding gum tissue. You may experience some discomfort if you do not take good oral care at home, and your gum tissue is inflamed prior to your dental visit, so it is important to see your hygienist regularly to maintain a good healthy oral environment.'

Well, of course this is the propaganda these predominantly female vixens would have you believe, in order for them to get their clutches on you. In my view, many seem to have a personality trait that compels them to cause pain as part of 'the treatment'. Do you have bleeding gums? You bloody will have by the time I finish with you. Teeth getting sensitive? Not to worry, when I scrape the tartar off I will crack the enamel and try to scrape that off as well. I suppose it has something to do with them having the ambition and rather sadistic temperament but not the skill to be a proper dentist which, possibly, makes them act as they do with cruelty and insincere kindness. They 'should' provide good care, but unfortunately many do not and I have concluded that for some obscure reason most patients seem to keep quiet about any mistreatment suffered at their hands. Also, of course, after what Lyndsay had done to old Hesaltine's dad I wasn't going to let her get near me!

We looked straight at each other for a moment and I could sense this odd and frightening psychological situation. She knew that I was aware something was not quite right.

Turning to go I headed for the double doors, but was suddenly grabbed from behind. Struggling I blurted out, "What the hell are you doing, woman!!! Get off me!" I felt something pushed against my shoulder an electric shock and then sudden disorientation and loss of balance. She had used some sort of stun gun on me and within a second her hands had my neck gripped in a vice like hold. Squeezing and squeezing the carotid artery, she knew exactly where to apply the pressure. My heart was now pounding in the desperate struggle, but unable to fight her off I began to feel the consciousness slowly leaving me as my brain was starved of oxygen. Within a few more seconds I had succumbed, becoming insensible and then blacking-out.

I cannot be sure how long I was unconscious, but when I awoke my vision was blurred and I was bound and gagged on the floor in the corner of old Hesaltine's treatment room. I blearily looked around and as my eyes began to focus I could see Hesaltine strapped firmly to the chair, his head was bound with some sort of tape to the head rest preventing him from moving.

"For god's sake Lyndsay, please just let me go. We can sort this out," Hesaltine pleaded as she was preparing an injection to use on him.

Grabbing a large dressing, she forced it into his mouth. "Now don't talk with your mouth full," she said sarcastically as she went back to filling the syringe. When this was done in a foul mouthed tirade she ranted on about those ungrateful bastards who complained about incompetence when she had tried to do her job maintaining their good, healthy oral environment, that they themselves had failed to do. She then, as I remember, called dentists in general and Hesaltine in particular a bunch of wankers for trying to make her lose her job over a few minor errors.

Hesaltine's nerves were tense and as I was looking at him I could see his fear and revulsion at what Lyndsay was about to do. She stared at him with what seemed to be a wicked delight and then conveyed to him calmly, even normally, the procedure that would be performed. "This is where I extract your teeth. Now will it hurt, I hope so," she said and removing the dressing from his mouth, commented, "Good lord man, it's a bloody dismal hole in there isn't it!"

Pulling up her face mask over her mouth she then grabbed his jaw and forcing his mouth open she stuck the syringe in and pushed the plunger down. After she removed the syringe, I could see Dr Hesaltine's eyelid starting to droop (due to the anaesthetic being injected in the wrong place in his mouth.) and his speech began to slur as he begged and pleaded with her to stop.

She picked up a pair of pliers all ready to pull his teeth out. I, meanwhile, was lying there in a state of some panic imagining what was in store for me. Sticking the pliers in and grabbing one of his teeth she started pulling and levering it to and fro then pulling at it, and I could see some watery blood starting to trickle out of

Hesaltine's mouth. Suddenly there was a loud crash at the surgery entrance. Lyndsay dropped the pliers down on the workbench and went towards the treatment room door to see what was going on. As she walked across I managed to swing my bound legs round and tripped her up. Falling, she hit her head on a portable instrument table and lay dazed on the floor. The treatment door then swung open and a couple of uniformed policemen pushed their way in.

"Thank god you have arrived," old Hesaltine dribbly spurted out.

It turns out that the surgery receptionist had arrived that morning only to be told the surgery would be closed and that she should put up a closed sign explaining it was due to a water leak. She did this and stuck it on one of the outside double doors. (The reason I did not see the sign when I arrived was that it had become 'hidden in plain sight'. Soon after it had been put on the door the tape holding the top of the sign had become unstuck and the sign simply flipped over. As it had been written on white card the plain back of the card just blended in with the white door and of course it was now at a lower height, making it easy to ignore or miss it.)

The receptionist was then told by Lyndsay that Dr Hesaltine had instructed her to go home, which she did, leaving them to lock up. I must have arrived before Lyndsay had a chance to lock the doors.

Luckily, the receptionist was suspicious that something was going on, as Lyndsay apparently had been acting 'strangely' after Hesaltine had given her a telling off. Apparently, she was quite worried about Lyndsay's behaviour and had decided to try to contact old Hesaltine on his mobile phone when she got back home, but with no success. She eventually decided to contact the police who sent over a couple of policemen to the surgery to investigate. While they were looking around the outside of the building one of them heard Hesaltine pleading for mercy, and to be released. They decided they had no option but to break in and rescue him from her clutches.

Conclusion

When I was interviewed by the police, they told me that Dr Hesaltine was not, in fact, the intended victim; it was actually Cynthia Curry. Apparently, Lyndsay had been having an affair with the MP and speaker of the House of Commons, the honourable Michael 'Squeaky' Bird. A pompous self-serving little man who would suck up to anybody to further his career, by all accounts. Michael Bird had used his position to gain access to MP's expenses fiddles and other rather shady dealings that went on in the Commons. He had acquired the nickname 'Squeaky' apparently because, like a rat, if he didn't get his pay-off he would ensure that the people responsible were 'informed' on to the papers or other authorities. I suppose you would say he was a kind of opportunistic blackmailer.

Lyndsay was a sort of slutty lap or pole dancer at the time, in other words a bit of a trollop, and was known under the name of Miss Fit, in those days. She apparently was eventually hoping to marry Michael Bird when he entered the Lord's and thus would become a respected lady.

However, things did not go to plan. Squeaky was 'usually' very careful not to get directly involved in the shady dealings so as not to incriminate himself if something did go wrong, but with Cynthia's 'arrangement' he got greedy and careless. When the dodgy deal became public, he was forced to resign and a police investigation subsequently got him a conviction and lengthy prison sentence. Many people, I understand, were glad to see him get what he deserved, and I think one press headline at the time was that 'He was a national embarrassment we were well rid of'.

Cynthia, on the other hand, had been much more 'careful' in the extent of her dealing arrangement in the matter and so was 'only' forced to resign.

With her hopes now in tatters, Lyndsay sought a way to make Cynthia pay for her role in Squeaky's downfall. To secure her hygienist job at the surgery, she did actually gain a Diploma qualification from Bristol University, but this was a correspondence course she did on the internet. That, combined with a few elaborate lies had secured her employment. Of course, having had no practical experience treating patients created a problem for her elaborate deception. It was lucky for Cynthia that Lyndsay was such a god awful hygienist and old Hesaltine had decided to dismiss her before she had a chance to attack her intended victim. Not so lucky for Hesaltine or me though.

Well, that's what you get with a woman's scorn I suppose.

Old Hesaltine recovered OK after the anaesthetic wore off, although he will need a bit of dental treatment to repair the damage done. And me, well when they set me free and I pulled off the gag the piece of tooth that was sticking out of my gum, and had prompted me to go into the dentists, had actually worked its way out. So, although my visit to the dentist was a bit of a horror story it was not all bad.

I wasn't going to bother, but I think that Cynthia certainly now owes me a nice little gift after what I have been through. "What did I do with that company card with her web site details on? Ah, here it is. Now I just type in the website address. Up it comes 'Cynthia C. Apparel'."

"Now what do we have here... um... sounds interesting."

"Just in Ermine Underwear. Highest quality from our exclusive supplier in China. Made with real 100% synthetic cat fur and at 'no' extra cost includes the cat flap and tail. Available in white and a wide choice of colours and sizes for the man or woman in your life. Also includes a purring noise-maker unit, fitted as standard for your partner's pleasure. A must for all discerning Royalty, Hereditary Peers and Lords and Ladies of all persuasion. Keep away from naked flames and other heat sources. Only £55.00 per pair plus postage and packaging."

CPSIA information can be obtained
at www.ICGtesting.com
Printed in the USA
BVHW042200310319
544207BV00012B/250/P